PUZZLE FARM

Susannah Leigh

Designed and illustrated by Brenda Haw

Series Editor: Gaby Waters

W9-ASF-461

About this book

This book is about Beth and Harry and their adventures on Puzzle Farm.

Puzzle Farm

Beth

Harry

We will be back in time for the fair!

Tilly, the Puzzle Farmer, and all her farm helpers have gone on a day trip to Puzzle Island. Beth and Harry are in charge of Puzzle Farm for the day. They have a lot to do as it's the farm fair in the afternoon. Some of their friends from nearby Puzzle Town have come to help them out.

Farmhands

Tilly

Puzzle Town friends

You will find a puzzle on every double page. See if you can solve them all and help Beth, Harry and the Puzzle Town people get everything ready for the fair. If you get stuck, you can look at the answers on pages 31 and 32.

The musical instruments

Tilly and her helpers have planned a surprise for after the fair. For this they will need their musical instruments. One instrument is hidden on almost every double page. Here you can see them all.

cymbals

fiddle

trumpet

bongo drums

banjo

harmonica

concertina

triangle

penny whistle

maracas

washboard

Patch
Patch is the farm puppy. Beth and Harry want to enter him in the puppy competition. But Patch has other ideas. He is hiding on every double page.

Can you spot him?

Purple puzzle mice
Puzzle Farm is the home of the only purple puzzle mice in the world. There is at least one mouse hiding on every double page. Keep your eyes open!

Early in the morning

On the day of the fair, Harry and Beth woke up early. There was a lot to do on Puzzle Farm.

First they had to feed the pony, the pig, the chicken, the duck and the rabbit. These were the animals that lived in the farmyard. But there was no sign of them. And where was Patch, the naughty farm puppy? Beth and Harry had to keep a special eye out for him.

Can you find all the farmyard animals?

Don't forget to look out for us, the purple puzzle mice!

Hay

Milking time

Beth and Harry fed the farmyard animals and then followed Patch's pawprints to the milking shed. Here they found Clive from Puzzle Town.

"I have to milk these cows," he wailed. "But I can't put them in the right milking stalls because I don't know their names."

"That's easy," said Beth. "Each cow looks like her name."

Can you see where each cow should go?

HATTY

16 SPOT

BIG SPOTS   SHAGGY   BELLE   SOCKS

Sorting out the animals

Outside the milking shed, Harry and Beth heard noises coming from the next field. They raced over and saw Mr Stamp the postman. He was looking at lots of different animals.

"Tilly told me to divide these animals into three groups ready for the fair," he said. "There's the spotty group, the feathered creatures and the animals with horns. But I can't work out which animals belong in which group."

Can you?

We don't belong in any of the groups.

In the greenhouse

Their next stop was the greenhouse. Tilly had given Harry and Beth special instructions to pick five flowers for the farm fair. She didn't mind what they looked like, as long as every flower was a different kind and a different colour.

Can you find five different flowers?

Whose babies?

In the field behind the greenhouse, Harry and Beth saw all kinds of animals wandering about. In the middle of them stood Mrs Bagel, the baker, scratching her head.

"These mother animals have lost their babies," she said. "I know the babies look just like their mothers, but I still can't match them up."

Can you match the baby animals with their mothers?

Stone steps

Their tasks were nearly finished when Beth remembered Tilly's best hat. It had been lent to one of the scarecrows and Harry and Beth had to find it in time for the fair.

The scarecrows were in a far away field surrounded by high walls. The only way through was the stone steps. But some of the steps weren't safe to climb and some were blocked.

Can you find a way across the fields to the scarecrows?

The scarecrows' hats

Beth and Harry arrived, puffing and panting at the field of scarecrows. There was a surprise waiting for them. All the scarecrows were wearing hats! Which one was Tilly's? Then Harry remembered that Tilly's hat was mostly red, and the flowers on it weren't blue or green. It should be easy to find.

Which is Tilly's hat?

Seven angry bulls

In the next field, Mr Tedd the toy shop man, was struggling to control seven angry bulls.

"I must keep these bullies apart," he cried. "But they all have to stay in this field. I've got these three special anti-bull poles to separate them. I've put one pole down, and now I don't know where the other two should go.

Can you fit the other two poles so that each bull is in a separate part of the field?

The farm fair

At last Beth and Harry finished all their tasks. Excitedly they set off for the fair. At the entrance they found Joe, the station master, looking very worried.

"The fair is about to start," he said. "My job was to meet Tilly. She's opening the fair. But she's not here and we can't start without her."

Can you see Tilly at the fair?

PONY RACE

FATTEST HEN CONTEST

LOST PETS

Smelliest Flower Contest

Prettiest Piggy

FRUIT STALL

WELCOME TO THE PUZZLE FARM FAIR

LOG SAWING

21

Tangled puppies

Beth and Harry breathed a sigh of relief. The fair had begun! Then they remembered the puppy competition. They raced to the main show ring, but Patch was nowhere to be seen. Inside the ring, the competition had begun. It was very confusing. Each contestant had two puppies, but the leads were all tangled up, and no one knew whose puppies were whose.

Can you untangle the leads and find out which puppies belong to which child?

LUCKY DIP

Prize-winners

At five o'clock everyone went to the judges' tent for the prize giving ceremony. But the prize-winners' list was lost. Now no one knew who should win which prize, or what competition they had entered. Beth and Harry looked at the prize-winners – the horse, the hen, the flowers, the cake and the pig. Then they thought back to all they had seen at the fair that day. Soon they knew which prize each had won.

Can you match the prizes to the winners?

The grand barn dance

But the fun wasn't over yet. That night, to celebrate the fair, there was a grand barn dance at Puzzle Farm. All the farm hands were back from their holiday. They played their instruments loudly as everyone danced the farmyard fling. But Mabel and Doris Green from the fruit and vegetable shop weren't smiling. They needed six red apples to finish making the fizzy farmyard fruit punch, and they couldn't see them anywhere.

Can you find the six red apples?

Animal surprises

When the music stopped, Harry and Beth heard another sound in the distance. They tiptoed quietly out into the dark night. The noise was getting louder and it came from the animal shed. Creeping nearer, they peered in through the window and saw a strange sight. The animals were having their very own barn dance! And at last Beth and Harry had found Patch.

How many animals have you seen before?
Where is Patch?

finding the babies

looking over the stone step

in the scarecrow field

near the greenhouse

near the bulls

outside the milking shed

Patch's dream

After the barn dance, Patch fell asleep and dreamed of the things he had done earlier that day. Look carefully at Patch's dream pictures and you will discover the story of the naughty puppy's day. If you didn't spot him on every page, these pictures should help you to find him.

at the farm fair

LUCKY DIP

escaping the puppy competition

ATCHOO

at milking time

in the farmyard

at the prize giving

Answers

Pages 4-5   Early in the morning
The farmyard animals are circled in red.

Pages 6-7   Milking time

Big spots   Hatty   Belle

Shaggy

16 spots

Socks

Pages 8-9   Sorting out the animals

feathers   spots   horns   horns   spots

feathers

Pages 10-11
In the greenhouse
You could choose several different combinations of flowers, but Beth and Harry chose these:

Pages 12-13   Whose babies?

E   A   b   D   B   f   a   C

g

c

d

h   G   F   H   e

Pages 14-15   Stone steps
The way over the stone steps is marked in red.

Pages 16-17
The scarecrows' hats
This is Tilly's hat.

Pages 18-19   Seven angry bulls
The two missing poles are shown in red.

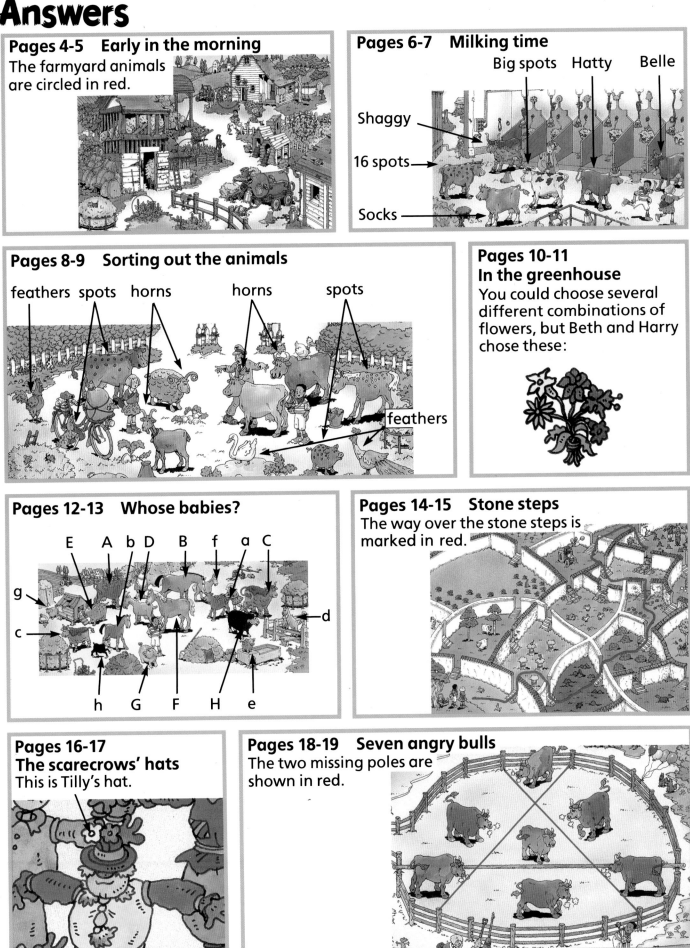

31

Pages 20-21   The farm fair

Tilly is here.

Pages 22-23   Tangled puppies

Pages 24-25
Prize-winners

Prize	Winner
Cup	Flowers
Shield	Cake
Blue rosette	Pony
Red rosette	Hen
Green rosette	Pig

Pages 26-27   The grand barn dance
The six red apples are circled in black.

Pages 28-29
Animal surprises

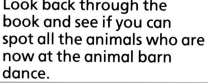

Patch is here.

Look back through the book and see if you can spot all the animals who are now at the animal barn dance.

First published in 1991 by Usborne Publishing Ltd, Usborne House, 83-85 Saffron Hill, London EC1N 8RT, England.

Copyright © 1991 Usborne Publishing Ltd.

The name Usborne and the device ♔ are Trade Marks of Usborne Publishing Ltd.

All rights reserved. No part of this publication may be reproduced, stored in a retrieval system, or transmitted in any form or by any means, electronic, mechanical, photocopying, recording or otherwise, without the prior permission of the publisher.

Printed in Portugal.

Did you spot everything?

Purple puzzle mice

Musical instruments

Pages	Purple puzzle mice	Musical instrument
4-5	five	banjo
6-7	three	triangle
8-9	five	cymbals
10-11	four	penny whistle
12-13	five	washboard
14-15	two	maracas
16-17	four	concertina
18-19	five	harmonica
20-21	three	trumpet
22-23	two	bongo drum
24-25	three	fiddle
26-27	three	
28-29	three	